DARK RETURN

A LANCE BRODY NOVELLA

MICHAEL ROBERTSON JR

This book is a work of fiction. Names, characters, places, businesses, and incidents either are products of the author's imagination or are used in a fictitious manner. Any similarities to events or locales or persons, living or dead, is entirely coincidental and should be recognized as such. No part of this publication may be reproduced, stored or transmitted, in any form, or by any means (electronic, mechanical, etc.) without the prior written consent and permission of the author.

ISBN: 9798335407625

Copyright © 2024 Michael Robertson, Jr.

Cover Design © 2024 Michael Robertson, Jr.

DARK RETURN

Lance Brody opened his front door and found a ghost staring at him.

This particular ghost was maybe four and a half feet tall and slender in build.

A child.

A breeze skirted the front yard, dead leaves prancing across the grass and down the sidewalk like crabs scurrying back into the ocean.

"Hi there," Lance said, trying to appear friendly as the ghost tilted its head back to take in all of Lance's towering height. Then he waited for the ghost to speak, to make its request.

Still, the ghost remained silent.

It wasn't until a miniature Spider-Man and Iron Man got in line behind the ghost that its mother nudged it in the back and said, "Go ahead, Grace. People are waiting," with the practiced patience only mothers have.

From beneath the white sheet of her ghost costume, in

which two holes for eyes had been cut out, a little girl's voice said, "Tricky treat," and she held out her candy bag.

Lance laughed. Tossed two fun-sized candy bars from the bowl he was holding into the girl's bag.

The mother grinned, but Lance could see she was tired. "She's said it that way all night, no matter how many times I've told her." She shrugged. Then, nudging Grace again, "Tell Mr. Brody thank you, Grace."

Grace was already turning to head back down the porch steps, but Lance caught a muffled thanks from beneath the sheet.

"Have a good night, Lance," the mother said.

Lance waved goodbye. "You too, Mrs. Saunders. Oh, and we should have a couple copies of the new Paul Tremblay at the library this Tuesday. Want me to put a hold on one for you?"

Alicia Saunders's face lit up brighter than the jack-o-lantern on the porch step. "That would be great! Thank you!"

"Sure thing," Lance said, then turned his attention to the two small superheroes who had stepped up to take Grace's spot on the porch, their bags held out with confidence. They said their trick-or-treats and Lance dutifully provided the goods, waving to the kids' parents who were standing back on the sidewalk, and thinking maybe Grace was on to something. *Tricky treat* sounded better.

When he heard the familiar and unmistakable sound of the Volkswagen Beetle's engine coming from down the block, he smiled and for a moment forgot all about candy and trick-or-treaters.

Leah was home.

The whine from the Beetle's engine got louder and Lance

watched as headlights appeared at the intersection at the end of the block when Leah made the turn onto their street, two dull and ghostly eyes glowing in the fading dusty-blue tint of dusk. The eyes grew larger as the car approached, and Lance watched as the car stopped halfway down the street, saw the outline of Leah's face appear as the driver's window rolled down. Heard her voice faintly carried to him on the evening breeze as she spoke loudly out the window, followed by the melodic notes of her laughter. Lance's gaze followed in the direction Leah was looking and found Alicia Saunders talking animatedly with her hands and then throwing her head back and laughing, too. At Alicia's side, Grace betrayed no emotion through her sheet, as if casual chit-chat was of no interest to those from the spirit world. Which, Lance knew, was not always the case. Some of those souls who are lost or trapped are only looking for a friend.

Lance grinned as he watched the two women's interaction come to a close, with Leah rolling up her window and Alicia taking her ghost's hand and heading up the next driveway for tricky treats. If people in Hillston liked Lance—and he liked to believe most of them did—they *loved* Leah. She'd started working part time for Mary Jennings at Downtown Joe nearly two years ago when Lance and she had returned to Hillston after that fateful night at Arthur's Adventureland, and it had taken no time at all before she was everyone's best friend. The stories—the *gossip!*—she'd brought home and shared with him were astounding.

Lance might have a way with the dead, but Leah sure was better with the living.

She reminded him of his mother in that way. Everyone loved Pamela Brody.

Everyone missed her.

Lance more than anyone.

The Beetle whined its way into the driveway and then shut off with a hiss of relief. The car had belonged to Leah's mother before she'd passed away, and had served them well since Leah had driven it away from Westhaven, traveling from Virginia to New England to Texas and back to Virginia, encountering rain and snow and extreme heat—not to mention ghosts and demons—without so much as needing air in the tires or a wiper fluid top off.

(Okay, it probably *had* needed an oil change, but such things weren't exactly pressing matters when one is trying to keep a hole from being ripped in the very fabric of the Universe, allowing all the creatures from Hell to come forth and devour humanity as we know it.)

A girl of maybe four or five wearing a Princess Peach costume was heading up the driveway behind the Beetle, clutching her father's hand. The father was dressed as Mario, and as Leah stepped out of her car and exclaimed, "Oh, you two are *adorable!*" the man beamed from behind his fake mustache. He pointed to his daughter. "She's never even played the games. Just likes the characters. I think I'm getting a bigger kick out of it than she is!"

"Well," Leah said, "What little girl *doesn't* want to be a princess and rule the Mushroom Kingdom?" She kneeled down to be eye-level with the girl and pointed to Lance. "You tell that silly man over there that I told him to give you as many pieces of candy as you want, okay?"

Princess Peach giggled and nodded fast. "Otay!" Then she pulled free from Mario's hand and rushed across the walkway to where Lance was standing on the porch and relayed the message.

Lance tossed three pieces of candy into the girl's bag and laughed. "She knows I can't say no to her," he told the princess, then looked at Leah and winked. "Is three enough?" he asked. The girl considered this for a moment, peering inside her candy bag. After apparently performing some calculations in her head, she nodded once. "Otay!"

When Mario and the Princess left, Leah finally made her way to Lance. She climbed the porch steps up to him. "Got anything sweet left for me?" she asked.

Lance said nothing.

He set the bowl of candy on the porch railing and reached for her, pulling her in close. He kissed her softly, smelling the scent of coffee and baked goods that always lingered on her after a shift at Downtown Joe—which was about as good of an aphrodisiac as Lance Brody could ever hope for.

They kissed once more, and then Leah turned around and moved to Lance's side. He put his arm around her and together they looked out across the yard, surveying the block. The jack-o-lantern on their front porch steps was the only decoration Lance and Leah had opted for, choosing the pumpkin a week ago from a stand at the Hillston Farmers Market and spending the evening carving it at the kitchen table while the original *Halloween* played on the TV in the living room. But while they had gone with a minimalist approach to their décor, several of the neighbors had gone all out; light and sound systems, fog machines, fake tombstones and coffins and skeletons, animatronic creatures and monsters. You name it, somebody on the block probably had it. It seemed like the neighborhood enjoyed decorating more for Halloween than they did for Christmas.

However, despite the neighborhood's enthusiasm for the season, what was decidedly missing from the sidewalks and street early on this Halloween evening, were people. Instead of the usual flood of pedestrian traffic and lines of vehicles slowly inching their way forward down the block, following their children house to house, tonight the neighborhood resembled more that of a ghost town—pardon the pun.

Mario and Princess Peach had moved on to the next house, and when Lance looked down the sidewalk in the opposite direction, he saw only two other sets of parents with their children. Three houses down, one of the over-the-top decorated yards flashed with eerie blue light as a skeleton stood guard halfway up the driveway, beckoning victims closer with an outstretched bone-finger, while *Monster Mash* played from a speaker. But no victims were present to fulfill the skeleton's wishes.

Dusk had just about given up the ghost now (again, pardon the pun), and the darkness of night fell over the block. Leah snuggled closer to Lance and said, "Geez, you were right. Everyone must have gone to the carnival."

Lance nodded. "Happens every time. I mean, it makes sense. If we had a kid, I'd probably suggest the same thing. Make it a one-stop shop sorta night."

He could feel Leah nodding against his chest. "Plus, there's funnel cake," she said.

"What more could we ask for?"

The carnival was one of those traveling types that could pop up in a field or a large parking lot seemingly overnight in any small town in America. It contained all the typical fare you'd expect: games, rides, two funhouses, food, and lots of lights and noise. This particular carnival apparently traveled up and down the eastern states during the summer and fall on some sort of rotating schedule, as they did not come to Hillston every year. But much to the delight of many Hillston residents, the years the carnival had Hillston on its schedule, it always arrived the week of Halloween. This was great because not only did they spruce up the usual attractions with spooky decorations, but they also gave out candy on Halloween night, allowing parents to bring their kids for a night of fun in one contained location and get all the treats they could stuff into their bags.

Lance, of course, had seen the carnival come and go several times during his life in Hillston, but this was Leah's first time. Despite their mutual affection for funnel cake, they'd both decided to not visit the carnival this year.

Two years might seem like a long time, but the sight of the Ferris wheel that spun lazily at the back of the carnival's layout brought forth memories of a night they were both still somewhat recovering from.

Several of the houses on the block, despite their ambitious decorations, had their porch lights off, their residents either not home or figuring there wouldn't be enough candy-hungry visitors to bother with buying a bag of candy and spending an evening getting up and down from the couch each time the doorbell rang. Maybe they were at the carnival themselves.

Lance picked up the bowl of candy from the porch railing and turned to head back inside. Leah followed, saying, "Let's keep the light on. We'll have more visitors. I can feel it."

Lance nodded. "Of course. The carnival's not for everybody. I'd hate for a parent to bring their kid out here and then find nobody was actually giving out candy."

Which was true. But what he was really thinking was, when Leah had a feeling, she was usually right.

They had that in common.

Inside, Leah said she was going to take a quick shower, so Lance sat in the living room recliner with the bowl of candy on the coffee table and picked up where he'd left off in the novel he was reading. He read a few pages, the sound of water running from the bathroom down the hallway providing soothing background noise, and then caught himself suddenly falling into a moment of surrealism—a gut punch of nostalgia and sadness that collided with hope and happiness, creating a cocktail of emotions that at-once confused and conflicted but also inspired and motivated.

He closed the book and set it on the coffee table next to the candy bowl, and then sat back and looked around the room. This was not the first of these surreal moments he'd experienced since he and Leah had arrived in Hillston after their showdown at Arthur's Adventureland, but they were growing fewer and farther between occurrences. The best he could describe the moments were a collision of two different lives, two different worlds.

The one-story ranch house Lance had shared with his mother all those years remained mostly unchanged. Much of the furniture was the same, the same plates and glasses and cutlery were tucked away in the kitchen cabinets and drawers, and the coffeemaker was still going strong. The bookshelves lining the living room walls still overflowed with the hundreds of books he and his mother had accumulated over the years, and Lance could scan the spines and covers and recall specific memories saved away in the caverns of his mind of exact scenes of his mother reading those titles—what she was wearing, where she was sitting, whether she had a cup of tea at her side. (Okay, maybe the tea was an easy one. Pamela Brody rarely, if ever, read a book at home without sipping a cup of tea.)

All these things were part of Lance's life before.

Before Leah.

Before Westhaven and Ripton's Grove and Sugar Beach and a roadside motel and a devil in the woods and Travelers Rest and an abandoned amusement park in Texas.

Before the Reverend and the Surfer.

Before his mother had sacrificed herself for him.

Before he started living his life after.

The moments he'd grappled with, like the one he'd just experienced while reading in the recliner, were times where he could feel himself slipping into the before life, as if his realities were shifting, and at any moment he'd hear his mother's footfalls on the porch steps outside and then watch her walk through the front door and greet him with a smile and her oh so familiar scent of lavender.

He had gotten to see her one last time that night at Arthur's Adventureland, her spirit even more bright and powerful and full of love than when she'd been alive—which, if you'd known Pamela Brody, you knew was simply astonishing. She'd told him not to grieve for her anymore, to go forward and live his life with Leah and enjoy every second of their time and the special bond they shared together. They'd done great things, and they were sure to do many more.

But still ... a boy will always love his mother. The sadness, though brief now, a pinprick instead of a laceration, would never fully fade.

The second half of these moments, the other reality into which he'd shift, was his return to the *after* and all the good that he had to be thankful for. He'd see the subtle changes around the house, decorations Leah had added—a few potted plants and framed photos and her own stack of books piled beside one of the bookshelves. He'd smell the scent of her shampoo and lotions, hear the now-familiar noises of her morning and nightly routines. See her car parked in the driveway as he looked out the window in the morning to check out the neighborhood, hear her laughter echo down the hallway as she chatted with a friend from Westhaven while laying on their bed. She always went to the bedroom or out on the front porch to talk on the phone, because she said she didn't want to get on Lance's nerves.

As if she ever could.

All these things warmed Lance's heart and he would find himself floating with happiness and gratitude, buoyed up from the deep and darkened waters he could sometimes sink to when he fell into the before life.

Neither was bad, the *before* or the *after*. Don't get him wrong. That wasn't the point. The point was that Lance wished more than anything both the before and the after didn't exist at all. He wished they both could simply coexist, meshed in harmony.

A beautiful *now*.

The water shut off down the hall and a moment later, the bathroom door opened and Leah padded barefoot across the hall to their bedroom, clad in a towel.

Lance shook his head. Smiled.

The *now* was as beautiful as anything ever had been in the history of the Universe.

And he would work hard to never forget that.

The doorbell rang, startling Lance fully into the present. He pushed himself out of the recliner, picked up the candy bowl, and headed for the front door. When he opened it, he found his boss from the library, Elizabeth Schickling, standing with her grandson half-hidden shyly behind her leg. The boy was wearing a Dallas Mavericks Luka Doncic basketball jersey that came down to his knees, and a white headband.

"Evening, Lance," Elizabeth said. "I figured you'd be home. Neighborhood's quiet tonight, huh?"

"Yes, ma'am. Everybody's at the carnival. Not really my speed right now, if I'm being honest."

Elizabeth nodded. "Ours either. Too much ... *everything*, for our liking."

Lance nodded with her.

Elizabeth Schickling was approaching seventy-five years old, but despite her wrinkled skin and thinning hair and physique that resembled the giant animatronic skeleton down the block, she moved lithely. Perhaps all those years roaming the rows of books and climbing the stairs at the Hillston Public Library had kept her legs strong and sturdy. When Lance had returned to Hillston after his adventures away, on a whim one day when he'd been feeling a bit down, he'd entered the library with no real reason other than it was a place that had always made him happy in the past. He had more memories than he could count of spending time there, both with his mother when he was younger, and then again alone as he'd gotten older and could make the walk himself.

When Elizabeth Schickling had spied him, she'd rushed to him, wrapped her bony arms around him, offered her condolences for his mother, and then asked him if he was looking for a job. Turns out, when Pamela Brody had passed away, the library had never filled her position. So, who better to take over for her than Lance?

He'd accepted the job on the spot. Between the library and coaching basketball at Hillston High School (another job that had somewhat fallen into his lap), he'd keep himself busy until...

Until the Universe needed him again.

"Liam! Are you Luka Doncic?" Leah exclaimed from behind Lance. "He's like, totally my favorite player right now!"

Liam's face completely changed, away with the shyness and full of a childish grin, and he slid out from behind Elizabeth's leg and opened his arms to let Leah scoop him up in a big hug. She spun the boy around in a circle as he laughed, and then she set the boy down and stood beside Lance.

"Hi, Mrs. Schickling. On trick-or-treat duty tonight, I see."

Elizabeth nodded and put a loving hand atop Liam's head. "It's our yearly tradition. Plus, I like the exercise."

Leah grabbed a handful of candy from the bowl and placed it in Liam's bag. "I hope I'm in as good a shape as you are when I'm your age."

Elizabeth Schickling leaned in close. "Want to know the secret?"

"Of course," Leah said, leaning in.

Elizabeth looked around, as if to check to see if anybody was watching. The street was deserted, which seemed to satisfy her. She looked both Lance and Leah in the eyes and then said, "There isn't one. Nobody has a clue what they're doing. Ever. Live *your* life, and don't worry about a thing."

Elizabeth cast a final look at Lance. Winked. "Pamela understood that better than most."

Lance said nothing.

Elizabeth bid them farewell and told Lance she'd see him at work, and then she and Liam were down the driveway and onto the sidewalk. Lance and Leah stood and watched them go. As the image of the woman and young boy faded into the dark, a porch light went off two doors down, and then another across the street.

Leah pulled her iPhone from the pocket of her sweatpants and glanced at the screen. "Wow," she said. "Looks like the fun's over and it's only a quarter past seven."

Lance nodded. "There'll be more kids next year. Besides," he nodded down the block in the direction Elizabeth and Liam had gone, "that was a good one to end on."

"So, we're callin' it? Light off?"

Lance surveyed the street once more, let his gaze travel along the sidewalk and houses. "Yes," he said. "Light off."

They went inside, and Lance closed and locked the front door. He flipped the light switch by the door into the off position, saw the glow from outside die out.

Leah had curled up on the couch, her hair was still wet, and it lay damp on the shoulders of her sweatshirt. Her feet were tucked under her as she used the remote to scroll through Netflix on the TV.

Lance moved to join her, plucking a mini Kit-Kat from the candy bowl and unwrapping it. Before he popped it into his mouth, he asked, "Trying to find us a film worthy of the holiday?"

She nodded, said, "Exactly," and glanced at him as he sat down beside her.

Lance stopped with the candy bar halfway to his mouth. He'd seen something in that glance. His gifts had always served him well when it came to reading people, picking up frequencies and undercurrents of unspoken truths and blatant lies and everything in-between. He could feel goodness radiating off people like heat, and the hairs on the back of his neck could prickle within range of Evil.

But none of that had anything to do with his understanding of Leah's glance.

They'd been together for two years now, living together for most of that time. The unspoken language they'd developed had nothing to do with either of their otherworldly abilities.

Lance could tell by just that simple glance that his girlfriend had something on her mind. Something she wasn't sure she wanted to talk about.

He ate his Kit-Kat while watching Leah continue to scroll through the movie titles on the screen. After another thirty seconds of her not picking a movie, he reached his hand out and gently placed it over hers that was using the remote.

She let her hand fall to her lap and turned to look at him.

"What is it?" he asked.

Leah looked away for a second, back to the television, contemplating her next words the way Princess Peach had contemplated whether three candy bars were enough. She sighed and set the TV remote on the coffee table and then leaned into the corner of the couch, wrapping her arms around herself and looking at Lance as she said, "I'm sorry. I thought I was over it, that I'd shaken it off, but seeing Elizabeth and Liam just now ... *feeling* the love between the two of them—you could feel it too, right? How strong their bond is?"

Lance nodded slowly. He'd felt it, sure, but he didn't know what a grandmother's love for her grandson had to do with anything right now. But if Lance was anything, he was patient.

"I guess..." Leah started. "I guess that warmth between them just contrasted so strongly with something I felt earlier today that it sort of, I don't know, triggered me a little."

Lance couldn't help it. He sat up straighter, his protective instinct awakening. "What happened?"

Leah settled him back down with a gesture. "Calm down. Nothing bad happened. It was just this intense sadness I felt coming from a woman at the shop today. I've seen her in a time or two before, but I didn't know her name. She was polite, but quiet. Didn't say much other than to order her latte and then say thank you when I gave it to her. She was trying to smile, I could tell. Like it was a lot of effort, but she was putting up a good fight with it. The entire time she was near me, I swear to you, Lance, the grief living inside her was suffocating. It chilled the air, made it hard to breathe. That poor woman is hurting like hell, and it bothered me the rest of the day."

Lance understood. Along with the gift of being able to pick up on other's emotions, and at times, their thoughts, came the burden of suffering second hand along with those who suffered. It was akin to a normal person swimming in the ocean and going through a cold spot, or a hiker walking through the woods and catching a whiff of something pungent—for better or worse. It could be a shock to the system. Lance had gotten used to it over the years, coming to the slow understanding that despite his abilities, he could not solve every problem for every person he encountered.

Leah's empathy and compassion toward others were some of the very first things Lance had noticed about her the day they'd met at her family's little motel in Westhaven. Those attributes had radiated off *her* and Lance had walked right into them, starting the process of him falling completely in love with her.

He could understand why an experience like the one she was describing had affected her so. And while Lance had had a lifetime to get used to these types of things, Leah was still adapting to her life with new Universal rules, new levels of senses that went well beyond those of most mortals.

"Do you know her name?" Lance asked.

"She paid with a credit card, so I read her name while she was putting the chip in the machine. Well, I could only see half of the first name, but it was easy enough to figure out. It's Rebecca Steel."

Now it was Lance's turn to feel a coldness creep across his skin.

"Oh," he said quietly.

"You know her?"

He nodded.

"I do. And I know exactly why she's hurting. Today of all days has to be one of the hardest days of the year for her."

Leah leaned forward, pulled her legs up and wrapped her arms around her knees.

"Why? What's wrong? Can we help her?"

Lance felt the coldness get replaced by the warmth coming from Leah, her passion for doing good for others. But he had to shake his head. "We can't," he said. "I already tried. It's too late now."

Leah reached out a hand and placed it on his knee. "Tell me."

Lance thought for a moment, reliving the memories in his head from several years prior. "Are you sure you want to know? It won't do much good to dig up a tragic past."

Leah didn't hesitate. "I do. I lived that woman's pain for just a few moments today, and it was more than enough. I need to know what could make her feel that way."

Lance knew he had to tell her. He knew *her*. If Leah didn't get the story from him, she'd get it elsewhere; a Google search would be all it'd take to get the gist of the story from any number of news outlets and Facebook posts.

But Lance ... Lance had lived part of it.

Lance leaned forward and plucked another mini Kit-Kat from the candy bowl and ate it thoughtfully, as if the sugar would help fuel him through the tale he'd have to tell. The tale of a person he hadn't been able to save ... even though he'd heard their cries for help.

He stared at the television screen, which was still full of images of the horror movies Leah had been scrolling through, thinking the scariest of them would still pale in comparison to the unimaginable nightmares of reality.

He was still staring at the screen when he started talking.

"Rebecca Steel had a daughter who was a year ahead of me in school. Chrissy. Her full name was Christian, but nobody had called her that since kindergarten. Anyway, Halloween night of my freshman year of high school, Chrissy disappeared."

Leah was sitting up with her legs crossed beneath her,

facing him, leaning forward so her elbows rested on her knees. Already invested. "Disappeared," she said. "You mean, taken?"

Now that it had resurfaced, Lance couldn't keep the sounds of Chrissy Steel's cries out of his head. He nodded and tried to quiet the noise. "Yes. Taken."

Leah bowed her head in thought, then looked up and asked, "By a person, or … you know, some other thing?"

Like Lance, Leah had also witnessed with her own eyes the things that lived beyond the veil, the monstrosities from the darkest pockets in the Universe. Demons from Hell. She understood the complexity of the word *Evil*.

"I'm not sure," Lance said, remembering the dark feelings that had accompanied the screams. The taunting that had seemed to seek him out and brag there was nothing he could do to save Chrissy. That he was too late. "Sometimes it's hard to tell where human nature ends and the otherworldly begins. Evil is"—(*Tricky treat*)—"tricky like that."

Now it was Leah who said nothing.

Lance took a deep breath. "The night she disappeared, I saw her in a dream. A … *strange* dream. It was quick, just a few seconds. My sleep had been dreamless until then, as far as I could remember when I woke up, but out of the blackness of my subconscious there had been a sudden pop of light, and I found myself standing in the vast black emptiness, staring directly at Chrissy Steel. She was wearing blue jeans and dirty Nike Air Max sneakers and a navy-blue fleece pullover.

"We just stared at each other for a few seconds, our eyes perfectly aligned, like we were trying to look into each other's souls. I'll never forget this part, because looking into Chrissy's eyes, I started to feel like I was looking at myself. And just as I was having this realization, there was another flash of light and suddenly I wasn't just staring at the Chrissy Steel in front of me, but I was *surrounded* by her. Clones that scattered around the blackness at various distances and sizes, and all of them ... they were screaming a silent scream, frozen in terror.

"Then I heard a loud knocking sound and the whole image washed away in another flash of light that I realized was the sun coming through the blinds in my bedroom as I woke up. There was another knock, and I heard my mother come out of her bedroom. I could still see Chrissy Steel's face twisted into a scream in my mind when I heard the front door open, and then the voice I knew I'd hear, asking..."

"Is Lance home?" Marcus Johnston's voice carried into the house.

Marcus, currently serving his first year as mayor, had been fresh into his law enforcement career as a young sheriff's deputy when Pamela Brody had chosen him as the first and only person with whom she'd share the secrets of Lance's special abilities. Lance had been just five at the time, and had used said abilities to locate the body of young Alex Kennedy, who had wandered away from home and drowned in the pond at a local Hillston park. Marcus and Pamela had gone to high school together, and there was no other explanation that Lance could ever reason as to why Pamela chose Marcus as their family's confidant other than she hadn't chosen him at all. Not exactly.

The Universe had chosen Marcus, chosen him to be the

Brody family's trusted friend, protector, to a certain extent, and most importantly, ally. Especially in those early years when Lance was a child with extraordinary gifts that had the great potential to draw the scrutinous and judgmental eyes of those less open-minded to believing in things that lay beyond the perceived simplicity of their human existence.

Hillston, Virginia, wasn't the deep south by any means, but growing up here as a Black man, and now having held certain positions of authority and power, Marcus Johnston knew a thing or two about scrutinous and judgmental eyes.

He was also one of the kindest, purest souls Lance had ever met.

Lance climbed out of bed and went down the hall to the living room, found his mother in her robe and slippers, closing the front door softly while Marcus stood to the side. Marcus wore jogging pants and a Washington Redskins hoodie. A team he said supporting was like being in an abusive relationship, but you keep hoping things will get better.

It was Saturday morning, hence the casual attire, but there was nothing casual about the look Marcus had on his face.

"I'll make some coffee," Pamela said, without asking any questions. She'd seen this scene play out enough times before to recognize it for what it was. As she passed by Lance, she reached up and squeezed his shoulder, and the love passed between them like sunrays.

When Pamela was in the kitchen and Lance heard her filling the coffee maker's water reservoir, he looked at Marcus, who still had not moved from where he was standing, and asked, "Chrissy Steel?"

At the mention of the young woman's name, Marcus closed his eyes and pinched the bridge of his nose. Sighed. "Shit." He opened his eyes and Lance could already see a bit of hope had drained out of them. "Here's the part where I hope you're about to tell me you know I'm here about the Steel girl because of teenage gossip. Word's gotten out already? Maybe some of her friends are texting, know where she is?"

Lance shook his head. "I had a dream. Just now. Your knocking woke me up." He told Marcus what he'd seen, about Chrissy Steel and all the versions of her staring at him across the blackness, their faces frozen in a scream.

Another sigh from Marcus. Another, "Shit." Then, "I guess we can rule out a runaway then. She had a fight with her mother last night, and we were all hoping she was just hiding out with a friend, blowing off steam."

Lance said nothing, which said everything Marcus needed to hear.

"Can you help?" Marcus asked.

Lance thought about all those faces. A multitude of scared young women crying out in terror ... begging for help. He couldn't hear their screams in the dream, but something in the Universe had created the connection between him and Chrissy. Had shown him what he'd seen as a, what, a warning? A clue? If that was the case, then maybe...

Lance had slept in basketball shorts and a long-sleeved Hillston High Basketball t-shirt. Without a word, he walked to where he kept his sneakers by the front door and tugged them on. Just as he finished, Pamela Brody walked out of the kitchen with a travel mug of coffee in each hand, little tendrils of steam escaping through the holes in the lids. She handed one to each of them and stretched up onto her toes and kissed first her son on the cheek, and then Marcus. "Go find her, boys. Bring that girl home. If anybody can, it'll be you two."

LANCE SHIFTED ON THE COUCH, turned to look at Leah, who still sat with her legs crossed under her and her elbows on her knees. Lance had never been able to sit that way, even when he was younger. Had never been flexible enough, and his legs always seemed too long for it to be comfortable.

"I've always remembered that," Lance said. "The way mom seemed so confident we'd save Chrissy."

All these years later, there still lingered the feeling of regret and sadness at letting his mother down. Of letting them *all* down.

Leah reached out a hand, seeing Lance's eyes grow unfocused as he drifted into his dark thoughts, and rested it on his knee. Her touch lightened his vision again, cleared his head. "You didn't disappoint her, Lance. You know that."

Lance tried to nod but only managed a small dip of his chin.

"You can't save everyone," Leah said. "You've told me that so many times, right? And Pamela knew that, too."

She was right, Lance knew. Of course she was. But...

"We were so close," he said.

"The mother called it in first thing this morning," Marcus said, backing his Mercedes sedan out of the Brodies' driveway. He paused to take a sip of coffee before shifting into Drive and heading toward town. "Chrissy had an early shift at the McDonald's over on Independence. She's worked there since the summer. The mother made it a habit to make sure the girl got up in time, because Chrissy had a tendency to sleep through her alarm clock."

Another sip of coffee as Marcus stopped at an intersection. A man jogging waved as he crossed in front of them. Both Marcus and Lance waved back. Habit.

"Anyway, when the mother—"

"Rebecca," Lance said. "Her mother's name is Rebecca. You know that."

Lance had met Rebecca Steel a few times at both the Hillston Sporting Authority where he worked, and the library.

"Yes, you're right. Sorry. It's hard to stop the '*official*' speak sometimes."

"Nothing official about what I do, so cut it out," Lance said. Took a sip of his coffee, then another.

Marcus smirked. "So, Rebecca goes in to wake Chrissy up this morning and finds the girl's bed empty. She's gone. And her car's still in the driveway. Which makes sense because—"

"Because they'd had a fight, and Rebecca took away Chrissy's keys."

Marcus turned his head as he slowed for the next stop sign. They were only a block away from the old brick buildings of downtown Hillston now. "You see all that in your dream?"

Lance shook his head. "No." Shrugged. "Just makes sense.

What's the worst thing you can do to punish a teenager with a driver's license? Take away the car."

Marcus drove on. "Well, that's exactly what happened. Rebecca grounded Chrissy. No car except for work and school. Two weeks. Took away her cell phone for the night, too. The last Rebecca saw her, Chrissy went into her bedroom and slammed the door. That was around eight last night."

"She snuck out. Window?"

Marcus nodded. "Yep. Single-story house, like yours and your mom's. Chrissy's window leads out to the side yard. Current theory is at some point between eight last night and five-thirty this morning, Chrissy climbed out the window and went..."

"Where?" Lance asked.

"I was hoping you'd know by now."

"I've been awake for ten minutes."

"I've been awake for three hours."

"Then why haven't *you* and the police found Chrissy yet?"

"We're trying, but *we* aren't psychics, Mr. Dreamwalker."

Lance opened his mouth to speak, then closed it. Sipped his coffee. "That's fair." Another thought hit him. "Where was Chrissy's dad?"

"Some tactical gear conference in Maryland for work. Sheriff's already spoken to him and the guy's driving back as we speak. Sheriff says he's pretty upset—said he never should have gone to the damn conference so soon after Rebecca had given birth."

This was news to Lance. "Rebecca Steel had a baby?"

Marcus nodded. "That's what I'm hearing. A baby boy named Connor."

The car was quiet as Marcus drove the next block, both of

them feeling the increasingly heavy weight of the fact a girl's life was probably at stake.

There's no probably *about it,* Lance thought, remembering those frozen, screaming faces. He tried to ignore the tingle of dread that crept up his spine. The one whispering they were already too late.

"What was the fight about?" Lance asked.

"All I know is what the deputy who went out to see Rebecca after she called in the missing person told me. The gist of it is apparently there was some big Halloween party last night and Rebecca told Chrissy she wasn't allowed to go because she brought home two D's on her report card, and she didn't unload the dishwasher like Rebecca had asked her to do twice that day. Chrissy did not respond well."

"Marlena Power's party," Lance said.

Marcus did another head swivel. "Were you there?"

Lance nodded. "Yeah. Most of the basketball team went. I didn't stay as long as most of 'em, though. Parties aren't really my thing. But you know, I try to pretend I'm normal sometimes."

"Was she there? Did you see Chrissy Steel at the party?"

Lance looked at Marcus like he expected better of his friend. "You know, I think you were sharper back when you were still in uniform. Don't you think I would have mentioned it by now if I'd seen Chrissy last night?"

Marcus sighed. "You're right. You're right."

"Give me some credit, man. I'm a Dreamwalker, remember?"

Marcus flipped on his turn signal and made a left, waving to a middle-aged couple holding hands coming out of Downtown Joe. The couple waved back and smiled brightly, the smiles of those who, in that moment, had not a care in the world. Lance envied them.

"That's an underrated film, by the way. The third *Nightmare on Elm Street*," Marcus said.

"That's Dream *Warriors*."

Marcus sighed again. "You're right."

They stopped at a traffic light, and on the corner of the sidewalk, a sign attached to a thin wooden post stuck in the top of an orange traffic cone read: CARNIVAL TRAFFIC, TURN RIGHT.

With the hand holding his travel coffee mug, Marcus gestured to the sign. "You and your mom get to the carnival this year?"

"Yeah, just for a bit. Got a funnel cake. Played some games."

Marcus nodded. "I performed my mayoral duties a couple nights. Shook hands. Got a fried Oreo."

"Just one?"

"That's classified information," Marcus said, making the right turn.

"Sure."

Marcus hadn't told Lance where exactly they were headed, but now Lance thought he knew.

"I'm guessing the police have tried talking to Chrissy's best friend?" Lance asked.

"The Sorento girl?"

"Emmy. Yeah. She was at the party."

Marcus nodded. "A deputy went over this morning. Rebecca Steel said she'd tried calling Emmy but hadn't gotten an answer, so she called the girl's parents instead. They said

Emmy got home at midnight, that's her curfew, but Chrissy wasn't with her and wasn't there now."

"I left the party around ten and Emmy was still there. I remember, she was making out with Kyle Hoffman on the stairs, and I had to literally step over them to head out. So, if Emmy saw Chrissy at all last night, it was between ten and midnight."

Marcus nodded. "Where's the Power girl's house?"

Lance gestured over his shoulder with his thumb. "Back on the other side of town, near the country club."

Marcus rubbed the side of his face. "I suppose that squashes the theory that she walked to the party. Too far, right?"

"Definitely. Especially in the dark." Then, "We're going to her house, aren't we? Chrissy's?"

Marcus nodded. "Yeah."

Lance did some distance calculation in his head. They were about a mile and a half from where the Steels lived, and most of that trek was a two-lane county road. There was a wide enough shoulder on either side to walk if you needed to (Lance had done it several times), but again ... at night, and alone, and as a teenage girl? Lance didn't think so. But if Chrissy was mad enough and determined enough and feeling rebellious enough, he wouldn't discount the idea all together.

"You said Rebecca took Chrissy's phone, but what about a laptop or and iPad?" Lance asked. "If she had one of those in her room, maybe she messaged a friend to come pick her up, meet her up the road here somewhere?"

"I'm sure the sheriff's department has thought of that, but I'll make sure. Shoot 'em a message once we're parked."

Then, "She wasn't dating anybody, was she? Her mother said no, but you know how kids are, right? All secretive and coy."

"Hey, I'm an open book," Lance said.

Marcus barked a laugh.

"But no, she's not dating anybody that I'm aware of, though we don't exactly hang in the same circles."

To the left, the few acres of flat field that butted up to the Willingtons' farmland, and also served as the carnival grounds and parking area, were empty except for one remaining food vendor hitching their trailer to the back of a large pickup truck, and lots and lots of trash and debris. Birds of all sizes hopped and swooped and darted about, gorging themselves on the smorgasbord of dropped and discarded treats.

Marcus looked out the window as they passed. "Crazy how they're just *gone*," he said. "It's kinda creepy when you think about it. You don't see them arrive, and you don't see them leave. They're just,"—he snapped his fingers—"here, and then,"—another snap—"they're not."

"I don't I know if it's creepy or just really efficient," Lance said, his gaze focused ahead, toward their destination.

Marcus actually seemed to consider this. Said, "It's creepy."

"How exactly are you planning on playing this?" Lance asked. "You're the mayor. I guess it makes sense for you to show up and start asking questions, acting concerned. But how do you explain my being with you?"

"Huh," Marcus said. He furrowed his brow. "I just assumed you could use your powers of telepathy and listen to my conversation with Rebecca from the comfort of the car. She doesn't even have to know you're with me."

"What is wro—" Lance stopped himself, saw the grin on Marcus's face lit up by the morning sun. He sighed. "Ass."

Marcus chuckled. "I did think about that already," he said. "Look, most people in town know we're close—me, you, and your mother. I'm just going to say I picked you up to go shoot some hoops at the Y, but then I heard about Chrissy going missing and I wanted to come check-in and make sure Rebecca knew I was going to make sure everything possible would be done to find her daughter."

"Enter me: The psychic, telepathic dreamwalker."

"I thought it was dream *warrior*. Are we back to dreamwalker?"

Lance sighed. "It's not a bad excuse for me being there," he said. "But I don't know what I'm supposed to—"

Lance's eyes went wide, and he jolted upright in his seat.

LEAH NOW LEANED back against the arm of the couch, legs stretched out in front of her, socked feet resting on Lance's lap. He rubbed them absentmindedly as he spoke. When he turned to look at her, Leah saw the pain of the memory in his eyes.

"We never made it to Chrissy's house," he said.

LANCE GRIPPED the sides of his head and squeezed his eyes shut. His movement had been so sudden that the seatbelt locked, tugging tight against his shoulder. He felt woozy, dizzy. He didn't drink alcohol, but the best word he could think to describe the feeling was *buzzed*.

"Lance?" Marcus said, concerned.

With his eyes still shut, Lance felt the inertia shift as Marcus eased on the brakes and the Mercedes slowed, which rolled in a fresh wave of unsteadiness in Lance's mind.

From behind them, a car horn blared angrily, and Marcus called the driver a bad word under his breath and then yelled, "Go around!" and Lance felt his balance shift again as Marcus pulled the car to the shoulder, the sound of an engine growling past them.

"Lance, what's wrong? Are you sick?"

Lance felt a gentle hand on his shoulder.

The buzzed feeling was abating, just a tiny bit. He took a couple of deep breaths, tried to suppress the nausea that had struck out of nowhere. His mouth felt dry and stale.

"I'm..." Lance tried, and then stopped. The car no longer felt like it was spinning in a slow, uneven spiral, so he risked opening his eyes. He thought his vision would be blurry, but he found he could see as clear as ever. "I'm okay," he said. "I just felt—"

Another jolt in his seat, this time not from sudden sickness but from surprise. A voice. Tiny. Soft. Afraid.

(Hello?)

The voice was female. Echoing in his head, lost in a cavern of uncertainty.

(Oh God, what the fuck?! Helloooo. Help! Help!)

The voice was fading now, but Lance heard enough. He may not spend his time in the same social circles as Chrissy Steel, but they'd been classmates off and on since elementary school.

The voice belonged the Chrissy.

(Help me! Please, somebody!)

Diminishing still, the voice faded as if the distance between Lance and it was increasing. Like Chrissy was...

"She's moving," Lance said, his own voice almost a whisper as he tried to establish himself back in the present, his own reality.

"What?" Marcus asked, his hand still on Lance's shoulder. "Who?"

"Drive," Lance said. "Now! Go!"

Marcus had known Lance long enough to know not to question the kid in times like this.

He drove. Accelerator smashed, tires spinning in the loose gravel and grass of the shoulder before biting the asphalt and squealing. The black Mercedes was like a bullet down the road.

Lance was thrown back into his seat as the car sped away, but his mind was thrust back into ... the other place. The place where Chrissy cried for help. The dizziness was returning some, and he could feel his own pulse quicken with panic, panic that was not fully his own, but partly fueled by another.

(Help meeeee!)

The voice was stronger again, loud and clearer.

"Marcus, keep going. As fast as you can."

Lance could feel a pull now, a magnetic energy that ... was *not* Chrissy Steel. It was not a spark of hope or the burning brightness of the pure and innocent and good that tugged at him, guided him, but instead the all-too-familiar aura of darkness that shrouded Evil.

The voice belonged to Chrissy.

And Lance now understood the pull came from her captor, the Universe's GPS coordinates to show him the way.

Lance let it in, let the pull grip his insides, feeling the sway and tug, feeling his stomach flip like he had gone over the drop of a roller-coaster.

The road on either side of the Mercedes was lined with tall trees now, and they'd cross the county line soon. Chrissy Steel's house was just around another curve in the road.

But they didn't get that far.

(Who the fuck are you? Get away! What the fuck are you doing? No! Please!)

"Left!" Lance screamed. Screamed for Chrissy.

Marcus stood on the brakes, rubber burning on asphalt as the car skidded. He ripped the wheel hard to the left and then floored the gas again, working the German-engineered machine for everything it had.

The voice was fading again, as was the pull.

"They're too far away," Lance said. "Too far ahead of us."

"Who? Who is it, Lance?" Marcus yelled over the rumble of the car's engine.

But Lance barely heard his friend. His mind was out there, searching, reaching for that connection that he felt rushing away.

He thought he had lost it completely. But then, just as he was about to tell Marcus ... *what*, exactly? ... a new voice crept through the shadows.

A man's voice.

(SHUT UP, BITCH!)

Then a scream pierced Lance's skull. Chrissy's scream. Full of terror and pain.

Lance felt his heart drop. There was a bright flash of light followed by immense darkness, sadness and grief splashing down on him in one giant wave that threatened to drown him right before his vision cleared again and his head stopped swimming and all sounds had ceased except for those of the Mercedes and his own breathing.

"Stop," Lance said, defeat in his voice.

"Stop?"

"Yeah ... stop."

Marcus eased on the brakes and again pulled onto the shoulder.

Lance looked ahead through the windshield. Watched a squirrel scamper across the road. A breeze sent a few leaves down from the trees. Fall in Virginia can be beautiful.

But right now, Lance saw no beauty in the world.

After a full minute of silence, Marcus finally spoke. "Lance?"

Lance turned to face his friend. Shook his head. "She's dead."

"Chrissy's body has never been found," Lance said.

The television screen no longer showed rows of movies from the Netflix app, but instead displayed a screensaver of a video shot from a helicopter flying high above a snow-covered forest. The view was supposed to be pretty, a calming, tranquil image, but in that moment, Lance found himself thinking that the scene on the screen looked cold and lifeless and empty. His dark memories tainting his present. His *now*.

Leah pulled her feet out of his lap, tucked her legs under her as she sat up. "That's terrible," she said, her voice soft.

Then, with some hint of optimism, "But ... if her body's never been found, maybe..."

Lance shook his head. "Leah, she's dead."

There was a beat of silence. The flyover video on the screen switched to a different setting, this one from beneath the surface of the ocean. Turquoise water filled with exotic fish. It popped with color and life, and Lance refocused, returned to his usual self. He'd beaten himself up enough before, back during that time when Chrissy had first gone missing. He'd *grieved* for her then—for her and the rest of the Steel family—but that was long ago, and he was too smart and too hardened now to think there was anything else he could do about it.

He cleared his throat and then shifted on the couch, turning to face Leah. "I can't explain it all—but hey, can I ever? All I know is what I felt when Marcus and I were driving that morning—that...*connection*—it was her. I felt her. No ... I *experienced* her in the final moments of her life."

Leah thought about this. Said, "You've done that sort of thing before, though, right?"

Lance shook his head. "Yeah. Now I have. But I hadn't then. I was, what, fifteen? A *kid*. That whole moment, feeling her, hearing her in my head like that, it ... it scared me." He took a deep breath. "It scared me, and I wasn't as strong as I am now. My," he sighed, "abilities, gifts, whatever ... were still developing, I guess. Still are, for all I know."

Which was true. Over those few months after Pamela Brody had been run down in the street by the Reverend and the Surfer, Lance had seemingly found new and strengthened abilities with each new task he was led to, including reliving the past both as himself and as others, and letting his mind—his *essence*—travel between multiple dimensions.

Freaky, right?

Leah reached for his hand and squeezed it. "I'll say it again, you can't blame yourself."

"I know," Lance said, lacing his fingers through hers. "I know. But it doesn't make things any easier, thinking about it now. I don't think I'll ever stop wondering if there was something we could have done differently, Marcus and me. That, and..."

He trailed off, let his eyes go unfocused as his memories tried to take hold again.

"And what?" Leah asked. She reached up and grabbed his chin, turned his face back toward her.

Lance allowed himself a moment to get lost in Leah's eyes, to fall in and let her catch him.

"Looking back on it over the years, replaying those few minutes in the car, there are times now where, after experiencing and dealing with some of the things I have, I wonder if Marcus and I really ever had a chance."

Leah tilted her head. "What do you mean?"

Lance ran a hand through his hair. "I mean, what if what happened that morning wasn't the Universe trying to help me find Chrissy, but instead it was—"

He felt a quick chill in his spine. Goosebumps dotted his arms as he remembered the man's voice that had shouted at Chrissy right at the end, and the subsequent darkness that had followed.

"—whatever Evil lived inside her killer connecting with me, to *taunt* me? To make me suffer through Chrissy's last moments and know there was nothing I could do to save her."

Leah said nothing. There was a time—her *before*—where she might have been able to convince herself that what Lance had just said was improbable; cruel, petty. But she now understood that such adjectives were just the tip of the iceberg of Evil's ever-expanding grip on humanity. Evil was limitless in its fuel to destroy joy, happiness, morale, and spirits. No task too big ... or too small. Evil *hated* those like Lance (and now her, too). Warriors for the army of Light. It took immense pleasure in their pain.

A car's muffler roared down the street outside, too loud, too fast. Leah thought it was probably a high school kid who thought all that noise and speed was cool, maybe on his way to a Halloween party—just like the one Marlena Power had thrown. The party which if Chrissy Steel had been able to drive to, she might still be alive.

Leah wondered if Rebecca Steel felt guilty because of this. If the poor women blamed herself, thought herself a terrible mother that had been too hard on her daughter and had driven her to meet her tragic end, to have her life cut unfairly and unjustly short. She wondered if her husband blamed her.

But Leah did not dare speak these thoughts aloud. Even though she knew the woman was not to blame, bringing this question into the world felt like doing Rebecca Steel a great disservice. The woman would have suffered enough by now without the need of any help from others.

"What happened after that morning?" Leah asked.

Lance leaned his head back against the couch and looked at the ceiling. "It went a lot like you'd probably expect.

Marcus and I drove around for another hour. We made three or four full laps around town, went out on a few of the county roads, drove by the high school, some of Chrissy's friends' houses, all to see if I could home in on her again, pick up on the connection I'd made before.

"At first, I told Marcus it was pointless, that I knew she was gone. But then, I don't know, I guess I started feeling desperate about the whole thing, which at the time I think I confused as feeling hopeful, and I thought maybe, if her killer had dumped her body nearby, there was a chance her spirit might still be around." He shook his head, managed a chuckle. "I don't know what I was expecting. I mean, did I think I was going to see her ghost hitchhiking on Route 19?"

"You wanted to help her, Lance," Leah said. "You always want to help. There's nothing silly about that. The world would be a better place if more people thought the way you did."

"Anyway, eventually Marcus took me back home. We sat at the kitchen table and mom made us more coffee, and we all went over what happened.

"Talking through it all, best we could figure what it all meant was this: Chrissy snuck out her bedroom window, started walking toward town, and somebody abducted her and drugged her and then eventually killed her."

"Drugged her?"

Lance nodded. "That had to be the dizziness I was feeling. The nausea and unfocused feeling that rushed into my head when the connection was first made. I think Chrissy had been drugged. Chloroform or something. Maybe even more than once. And then when she woke up and started making a racket, she was murdered." He paused and took a breath. "What was done to her all those hours between her abduction and murder ... I don't know and don't want to know.

"What we do know, or rather, what we highly suspect, is that there were at least two people involved in whatever happened to Chrissy."

"Why two?"

"Because of the feeling I got that she was getting further away from Marcus and me while it was happening. I think she was in a moving vehicle, too. Probably a panel van or some sort of moving truck. Maybe even a semi. Somebody had to be up front, driving, and somebody else was back with Chrissy."

Leah thought about this. Wasn't sure she liked it. "That's a big assumption."

Lance shrugged. "Maybe. But it feels right. I can't explain it any other way."

Leah nodded. "Sure. Okay, so she leaves her house and starts walking. *Nobody* saw a young girl walking alone along the side of the road that night? None of her friends had any idea where she might be headed?"

"Ah," Lance raised a finger in the air. "There was that. The question of if Chrissy was dating anyone came up, and while her friends initially said no, a guy named Marshall Lewis showed up to the sheriff's office the next day and confessed that he and Chrissy had been *talking*," (Lance made air quotes), "and *hanging out*," (more air quotes), "secretly for a few weeks leading up to her disappearance. When this info came out, Emmy Sorento, Chrissy's best friend, finally admitted this was true. She was the only person Chrissy had told."

"Why the big secret?" Leah asked. She pushed herself off the couch and then sat on the coffee table, facing Lance.

"Because Marshall Lewis was twenty-one years old and lived a couple towns over in Forest. Remember, Chrissy was only sixteen."

"Ohhhh shit."

"Yeah. Apparently, they met when the Hillston football team played Jefferson Forest on the road. Anyway, Marshall swore he had no idea what happened to Chrissy, but he did tell the deputy who took his statement that he knew Chrissy was supposed to go to the Halloween party, but he told her if she wanted to come have a better time with him, he'd be at the carnival. He'd been trying hard to encourage her, but he figured she wouldn't ditch the party for him."

Leah stood up, started pacing in front of the coffee table. She grabbed a Butterfinger and unwrapped it, but didn't eat it.

"And he never saw her at the carnival?"

Lance shook his head. "No. Marshall said he stayed till around eight-thirty, got bored and hadn't heard from her—he didn't know Chrissy's phone had been taken from her—and then got in his truck and drove to a different Halloween party some of his friends were at in Forest. His story checked out. People confirmed he was there."

Leah popped the Butterfinger into her mouth. Chewed and then spoke. "Doesn't mean he didn't have anything to do with it, though, right?"

"He didn't."

"How do you know?"

Lance smiled. Leah was in that mode. That *determined* mode.

"Because Marcus brought me to the sheriff's station when Marshall gave his statement. I watched the guy through the two-way mirror as he told his side of things. I felt nothing but fear and sadness coming off the guy. He was both terrified for Chrissy and for himself. I think he really did like her. A lot. Despite the ... shall we say, complicated nature of their relationship."

"You mean the illegal nature?"

"Yes. That."

Leah sat down again. Looked down at the carpet while she thought. Finally, she looked up and asked, "So that was it? The end?"

"Pretty much. Marcus made sure the sheriff and his team were doing all they could. All the news outlets were covering it. *Anybody who has any information at all, please come forward*, all that normal stuff. All Chrissy's friends were questioned again. Rebecca and David Steel offered a reward, but money can't find answers that aren't there. School was weird for a while; a lot of people were freaked out, a lot were spreading rumors, but mostly everything just felt ... less important than before. It was like, for a lot of the students, Chrissy's disappearance was the first taste they'd had of the real world. The first time they realized they might not be invincible. The whole *It won't happen to me* had happened to one of them. It shook things up. For a while. But eventually..."

"Life goes on."

Lance nodded. "It does. And it did. The worst part is that while the community eventually came around to the realization that Chrissy was likely dead, Marcus and I knew it from the beginning. But what could we do? What could we say? I had my own secrets to protect, and nothing I had felt that morning would have done any good. It would have only made me sound crazy."

Leah sighed. "That poor, poor family."

"I think they've tried their best to move on," Lance said. "I didn't use to see David much, but I did see Rebecca from time to time in the years after it happened. I've actually seen her in the library once or twice with Connor since I've been back. I can feel that sadness in her, but today, on the anniversary of Chrissy's disappearance, I'm sure you felt the full strength of her grief as the memories had to be impossible for her to ignore. Heck, this year, even the—"

The doorbell rang.

The noise startled both of them, and the living room seemed deathly silent after. Both Lance and Leah turned their heads toward the front door.

The television shut off a second later, casting the room in almost complete darkness. The only light came from the end table lamp that Leah had dimmed low before settling in with the plan to watch a scary movie, and…

"I thought you turned the porch light off," Leah said.

Through the edges of the blinds that covered the windows on either side of the front door, came a warm glow from outside near the porch.

"I did," Lance said. "I'm positive."

He stood from the couch and grabbed the candy bucket from the coffee table, but as he made his way across the living room and to the foyer, his eyes never left that glow. The closer he got, the more it seemed the light was slowly flickering. *Pulsing,* as if struggling to stay lit.

He reached the front door and eyed the switch for the

porch light. It was down. The off position. Just like he knew it would be.

When he grabbed the doorknob, the hair on the back of neck prickled with a buzz of energy. He twisted and pulled on the knob. The door opened.

Two people waited on the porch. Rebecca Steel looked tired—*exhausted*, really, a look that brought to mind Lance's memory of her when the Steels had pleaded Hillston for help at the Sheriff's press conference several years ago—but she did her best to force a smile when Lance opened the door. "Hi, Lance."

Lance couldn't speak.

"We got a late start—wasn't sure we'd come at all, actually—and almost nobody is still giving out candy. We were driving by, and I saw your light turn on, so I thought we'd give it a try."

Rebecca was standing a couple feet back from the door. In front of her, stood the woman's dead daughter.

Chrissy Steel's ghost was the version of her frozen in Lance's mind—the sixteen-year-old who'd once walked the Hillston High School hallways alongside him. But while Lance and his other classmates had eventually walked out of those hallways and out into the rest of their lives, Chrissy Steel did not. Instead, she'd left her home on Halloween night and had not been seen since.

Until now.

She wore blue jeans and a navy-blue fleece pullover. Dirty Nike Air Maxes. The same outfit she'd worn in Lance's dream the night she'd gone missing. Looking at her now, Lance was taken aback at how much she looked like just a kid. Sixteen feels so old when you're that age. You wake up one day with a driver's license and take your first drive to the store alone and buy yourself lunch at a drive-thru somewhere and think to yourself, *This is what adulthood feels like. I'm in charge of my life now.*

If only we knew what adulthood was really like, kids would never be so eager to grow up. They'd walk those high school halls forever.

A kid, Lance thought. *A kid, and somebody killed her.*

Chrissy's image was a nearly translucent figure that transposed itself overtop the body of Connor Steel, her little brother, now nine years old and outfitted as Dracula and standing just in front of Lance with his candy bag held in two hands down at his knees. Her image blurred and buzzed, came into full focus one second, only to fizzle out again to be barely noticeable, bringing Connor's features into full color and detail. In ... and out. In ... and out. She seemed to—

She's pulsing, Lance realized. *She's pulsing in sync with the porch light.*

It was then he understood. Chrissy Steel's ghost was using all the energy she could squeeze out of the Universe to be here. *She* was the one powering the porch light. She'd turned it on to bring her mother and brother here, to Lance.

She still needs me, Lance thought.

"Lance?" Rebecca Steel asked, her voice more concerned now.

But Lance found he couldn't look at the woman, couldn't pull his eyes away from Chrissy's. Felt his heart ache for the sadness in them.

The porch light dimmed, nearly gone now, and with it Chrissy's image faded almost completely into the darkness of night.

Lance almost called out to her, but then the porch light burst back to life, brighter than it had any right to be. It produced a low hum that followed a crescendo to a high-pitched whine. Lance flinched at the noise, but then saw Chrissy's eyes grow wide, watched as her image popped back into existence one final time, her face strained and her eyes begging. Her mouth opened, and Lance was overwhelmed with the memory of that terrible dream where he'd witnessed several versions of Chrissy locked in silent terror. But this time Chrissy's face wasn't frozen. Her lips kept moving, pursed together tight at first—

(mmmmmmmm)—and then opening again—*(mmmmm-meeeee)*—and then puckering into an O shape—*(mmmmm-meeeeeeroooo)*.

The porch light whined louder. The metal enclosure began to rattle and vibrate.

Lance closed his eyes. Tuned it all out. Focused on Chrissy. Searched for what little energy she had left to pull from and latched onto it. He swam through the waves of darkness, called out for her and—

He found her.

(MIRRORS!)

Chrissy's voice boomed in his head.

Lance's eyes shot open. The light bulb inside the metal enclosure exploded with a *POP!* and a tinkle of shattered glass.

Everyone jumped.

Chrissy was gone.

Rebecca Steel put a hand on Connor's shoulder and pulled him back. They were hardly more than silhouettes in the darkness left behind by the broken light. Shadows on top of shadows.

"Sorry," Lance finally managed to say, his voice partially trapped in this throat. "That bulb's been acting up lately." He held out the candy bucket to Connor. "Here ya go, man. Take what's left. I think you guys will be our last visitors tonight."

Connor looked up and over his shoulder to his mother's face. Rebecca looked at Lance for a beat, then to the busted light. She nodded.

Connor stepped forward with his bag held out, and Lance dumped all the candy from the bucket inside it.

"Thank you," Connor said. Then, "Mom says you knew my sister. Back before we lost her."

"*Connor*," Rebecca Steel reached for her son.

"She says Chrissy liked to watch you play basketball. That she thinks Chrissy had a crush on you but was always too afraid to tell you."

"*Connor, that's enough!*"

But Connor did not think it was enough. "When I grow up big like you, I'm going to go find Chrissy. Then she can come back and tell you she has a crush on you. Is that okay?"

Lance ... said nothing.

She was right here, kid. And I think she told me what she needed to.

He looked at Rebecca Steel, watched as she wiped tears from her eyes.

Lance bid them a good night, watched them make their way down the driveway. When he went back inside, he wrapped Leah in a hug that he never wanted to end.

Then he told her what had happened.

"Why now?" Leah asked. "Where has she been all this time? I mean, if her ghost was still around, why did she wait so long to come find you?"

She was pacing again, talking with her hands, energy reignited.

Lance was standing behind the couch, halfway to the kitchen, wondering if he should make some coffee. He wanted the coffee (okay, he always wanted the coffee), but part of him suddenly felt very tired. Bed was where he really wanted to go. As if the encounter with Chrissy had drained his own energy, used up his resources.

"I don't know," Lance answered. "I ... I don't think she was *supposed* to be here."

"What do you mean?"

Lance pointed to his left, toward the front door. "The light," he said. "The energy she had to use. Chrissy had to fight to be here, to cross over something ... or escape something. Wherever her spirit has been trapped or—"

He stopped. Stood up straight.

"What is it?" Leah stopped pacing. Stared at him.

"Or whatever she's attached to."

Realization hit Leah, too. "You mean *whoever* she's been attached to."

Lance nodded.

"Her killer."

"I think so," Lance said. "Whoever murdered Chrissy is close. In town. Maybe even for the first time since her death."

"Why would she be attached to her killer?"

Lance took a deep breath. Tried to formulate his answer.

"Don't think of her killer as a human being. Think more of the Evil thing that lives *inside* the person. A dark soul, the driving force behind their kills. If..." Lance thought some more, then continued, "If this darkness was strong enough, it might be collecting the souls of its victims. Keeping them like trophies. Maybe feeding off them for strength. Creating a sort of," he shrugged, "isolated version of Hell for them."

Leah didn't speak. Shook her head at thoughts of the nightmare Lance had just described. Lance almost turned to the kitchen for that coffee, but at the last moment, Leah's voice stopped him. "So, how did she get away? I mean, you're the obvious target if she *could* get away, but even so, the killer being close is only half of it, right? If she had the power to escape, why wait until now?"

Lance was quiet for a long time, lost in thought. It was a good question. If Chrissy's soul could have escaped before, she would have. No one would linger in torment longer than they had to. Which only meant that she hadn't had the strength before. She must have needed help, something to strengthen her, give her an extra boost, so to speak. Something to help carry her past the gates of her prison, if only temporarily, before eventually getting dragged back.

Something strong.

Something the Evil that was her captor would have trouble fighting off. Something that could blindside it. Something like...

"Connor," Lance said. The reason Chrissy's ghost chose to overlay itself atop her younger brother as opposed to simply appearing beside or behind or in front of him. "Her family." He looked at Leah, fresh understanding on both their faces. "The bonds of love."

Leah brought a hand to her mouth, a shocking thought hitting her. "If she had to cling onto Connor for escape, does that mean she would have had to have been close to him to begin with? Like, physically close?"

Lance wasn't sure. He never had all the answers. Could only work off his own experience, and what secrets the Universe shared with him as needed. But it made sense. "It's possible," Lance said. Understanding where Leah was headed. "Which means Connor Steel has probably been in the presence of his sister's killer and never had a clue. Rebecca, too, for all we know."

Leah shook her head again. "Terrible."

Lance agreed.

"And what about the word she said? *Mirrors*."

That was the million-dollar question. The one that seemed to weigh heavily with exhaustion on Lance's mind. For Chrissy to have fought so hard to reach him, knowing that her time and strength were so limited she could only deliver a single-word message to him, the word must carry tremendous meaning.

Obviously.

But what?

There was something there, something just out of reach in his mind. Two ends of a connection that could see each other but not quite make contact.

Instead of going to the kitchen for coffee, he walked around to the front of the couch and sat down. "I need to think," he said. "It's right in front of me, I just have to see it the way it wants to be seen."

He leaned his head back against the cushions. Stared at the ceiling. Felt his eyes growing heavy.

He was only half aware of Leah kissing his cheek and whispering that she was going to the bedroom. She'd be there if he needed her. He felt himself nod and tell her he loved her.

"I love you, too." Her words followed him into sleep like the sweetest of lullabies.

∼

"Are you ready to go?"

Lance opened his eyes and found himself still on the couch in the living room, but something was off.

It's too bright. Too bright to be night still. The realization sank in as Leah asked another question.

"We walking or driving? It's warm enough I think we can walk. As long as the wind stays down."

Lance turned his head and found Leah standing by the front door. She was wearing what he'd seen her in last, the sweatpants and sweatshirt. No shoes on, just her socked feet. But she had her hand on the doorknob, ready to leave.

Lance stood, drawn to her. "We can walk," he said. "I'm always up for walking."

She nodded and smiled. The sunlight that shouldn't be there came through the front windows, bathing her in white light. Angelic.

When Lance reached her, she took his hand in hers and pulled him forward, opening the door. The light outside was blinding, and Lance had to raise his free hand to shield his eyes as he followed Leah across the threshold.

He stepped out, expecting to feel the wooden planks of the porch, but instead he felt earth beneath his feet, the soft crunch of dry grass. Behind him, the door slammed shut, and he spun around. As he did, his vision instantly adjusted, like somebody had dialed down the sun, and he found the door —and the entire house—gone. In its place was the view of the backside of a row of downtown Hillston buildings. In the distance, he could see the top of the courthouse towering above all.

He knew exactly where he was.

The sound was piped in then, as if somebody had flipped a switch—music, the din of laughter and conversation, the occasional squeal of delight or fright, grease sizzling, oil frying, a muffled voice booming from a speaker in the distance, the hum and whir of machines and generators, electronic beeps and chimes. The air was redolent with scents of fried and smoked and grilled food, a cloying aroma of sugar laced among it all.

Lance turned back around and saw the carnival. The layout was exactly the way he remembered it from the last time he and his mother had come here. To his right were the rows of games—the ring-toss and balloon-pop and basketball-shot and knock-over-the-cans among others—and straight ahead he saw the funnel cake hut next to the cotton candy booth. More booths and food- carts and trucks stretched deeper into the field, and beyond them, the rides, where everyone could pay cash to try to not puke as they rode such classics as the Tilt-o-Whirl and the Mouse Trap coaster. And looming over it all in the distance, just like the courthouse spire, the Ferris wheel spun in a lazy circle.

Despite the sounds of life, despite the movement from the rides, despite the air thick with the smells of food, the carnival was dead.

Lance could not see a single person, as if the entire scene was nothing more than a—

(Dream)

—mirage. He turned to ask Leah if she saw anyone, when he realized she was no longer with him. He didn't know when he'd lost hold of her hand, but figured it must have been during his moment of confusion as he'd spun around to look for the door that was no longer there.

Panic almost seized him, and he was about to call out for her when he turned back toward the carnival and saw her waving to him from off to the left.

He didn't hesitate, began jogging toward her. As he moved, he took in the massive shape Leah was standing in front of, the structure's shadow looking as though it reached for her.

Two stories tall and as long as a semi-truck's trailer, the carnival fun house was painted with all variety of bright and vibrant colors, decorated with human-sized imagery of clowns and jokers. A red, white, and blue retractable awning stretched out in an attempt to look like a patriotic circus tent. *God bless America, and God Bless the Clowns.*

Lance watched his world darken as he entered the fun house's shadow, sidling up beside Leah.

What's going on, he was about to ask. But he didn't speak, noticed Leah wasn't looking at him but was instead staring straight ahead at a sign attached beside the fun house entrance. White with black hand-painted lettering advising patrons of all the *fun* they'd encounter inside the walls.

Lance scanned the list: *The Clown Hall, The Upside-Down Room, The Tilted Corner, The Moving Staircase, The Maze of—"*

Lance felt ice in his blood.

The Maze of Mirrors.

He quickly turned to Leah, but again she was gone. Instead, he found his mother.

Pamela Brody smiled at her son, and the shadows receded. "Go," she said.

∼

LANCE'S EYES fluttered open and the living room ceiling came into view. Before he could even sit up, he heard a door open from down the hall, followed by Leah's rapid footsteps.

"The carnival!" she said. "The Maze of Mirrors!"

Lance stood up quickly—too quickly, the room doing a little jig before settling. "You saw it too? The dream?"

Leah nodded, already moving toward the door, grabbing for her sneakers. "It was so weird. Like I was watching myself, but I was also inside my own head, you know?"

"Did you see my mom?" Lance asked, still feeling some of the warmth from his mother's presence in the dream bleeding into reality.

Leah stopped with her shoes and stood, looked at him. "What? No, I didn't see anyone except you. The place was like a ghost town." She paused. Thought, "What does that mean? If you saw her, I mean."

Lance moved to join her at the door, his mind and body feeling energized. Strong and confident and determined.

"It's confirmation," he said. "I don't think mom ever truly let go of Chrissy Steel, either."

Leah saw the look in Lance's eyes and quickly tied her other shoe. Pulled her phone from her pocket. "What the heck?" she said, staring at the screen.

"What?" Lance already had his hand on the doorknob.

"It's almost four in the morning. How is that possible? I feel like I only dozed off for a few minutes."

Lance opened the door and the cool night air rushed for them, the street dark and silent and still. "It means the Universe woke us up exactly when we needed to get started," he said.

("Go.")

"We have to go right now."

∽

LEAH DROVE and Lance used her phone to text Marcus Johnston (It was easier to text on her phone versus Lance's flip-phone), telling him to get some sheriff's deputies and head to the carnival grounds immediately. Lance thought about calling instead of sending the message, but figured Marcus would try to slow him down, stop him from doing something *"stupid"* and getting himself hurt. Despite all Marcus's understanding and respect for what Lance could do, the man's paternal-like protectivity could still cause some untimely hiccups in Lance's actions. And something about this current situation told Lance he didn't have time for untimely anything.

No surprise, Marcus texted back almost immediately: On it. What's this about?

Lance texted back just a name: Chrissy Steel.

Now Marcus did call. Lance sent it straight to voicemail. Texted: Get them there now. The fun house with the mirror maze.

Marcus sent back an angry-face emoji, but left it at that.

Leah drove through the darkened streets of Hillston, and before she made the right turn to go the final half mile or so to the carnival grounds, Lance told her to kill the headlights. She did. When they were a hundred yards out, they saw the carnival grounds were mostly dark and still now that all the festivities were over. The only movement and lights they saw were headlights from trucks being hooked up to trailers and booths, and flashlight beams crisscrossing everywhere like shooting stars as workers prepared themselves and their equipment to roll out and head for the next town.

"Park here, on the shoulder," Lance said.

Leah pulled over.

Lance pulled his sweatshirt hood over his head, grabbed the door handle. "Text Marcus," he said. "Tell him exactly where you are and to come find you when he gets here. Knowing him, he'll be here before the sheriff's department. If I'm not back, tell him to come get me in the fun house."

Leah started to protest. "I don't want to just sit here and do nothing! I can—"

"You're not doing nothing," Lance said. "You're our roadblock."

"What?"

Lance pointed out the windshield, where the sleeping beast of the fun house lay in wait. Even from the car, they could see there was a large pickup truck, maybe a Ford F-350, hooked up to the front of it, ready to tow. "If that thing starts moving, park this small yet mighty Beetle sideways in the middle of the road and block their way."

Leah blinked. "They could just plow right over me."

Lance shook his head. "They won't. If this guy's been abducting and killing young girls in secret all these years, he's not going to cause a scene by playing monster truck on a public road."

"And if they just go around me?"

"Let them. Your only job is to slow them down in case they move out before Marcus and the deputies get here."

Leah nodded. "Okay ... Okay, yeah. I get it. Yes."

Lance leaned over the center console and kissed her.

"Wait," Leah said. "Here, you'll need this." She reached over and opened the glove box. Retrieved a small flashlight no bigger than a roll of quarters, and handed it to Lance. "Daddy says to always keep a flashlight in your car and check the batteries regularly. I'll be honest, I haven't checked the batteries since he gave it to me."

Lance slid the flashlight into his pocket.

"Be careful," Leah said.

"Always."

"Liar."

Lance got out of the car and closed the door.

Leah watched as he moved across the street and into the field like a phantom in the night.

∼

LANCE COULD FEEL the pull as soon as he stepped foot off the road and onto the trampled grass of the section of the field that had been used as the patron parking area. The hairs on his neck prickled, a buzz at the base of his skull. An internal compass pointed him right at the fun house.

He hunched down as he moved quickly through the grass, trying to lower his tall frame, stay close to the ground. It was eerily quiet, his breath sounding loud in the night.

Closer now, voices could be heard, random chatter from workers. A truck engine started, and a new set of headlights blossomed, lighting up an area fifteen yards to Lance's right. He jumped to the left, putting more distance between himself and the truck's beams, but kept moving forward as fast as he dared.

Fifty yards from the big F-350 hitched to the fun house, Lance felt the cold. Not a chill from the cool fall temperatures, but a coldness he was all too familiar with. The coldness of death and Evil, pain and sadness.

It was this coldness that pulled him toward it, guided his compass needle. It was powerful.

Most of the movement and lights were on the opposite side of the grounds, toward the food and game booths, but just down from the fun house, Lance could now see the darkened shapes of four men standing around the back of another pickup truck hitched to a flatbed trailer stacked high with what looked like sound equipment cases, the type of locking black boxes you'd see unloaded and loaded for a music concert. Two of the men were standing on opposite sides of the truck bed, talking over it, and the other two were squatted down near the hitch, flashlights examining something.

Lance crouched lower and crept toward the front of the F-350 that would pull the fun house. He reached the front passenger side and crawled around the front of the truck, peering slowly around the driver's side and looking back to the fun house entryway. The red, white, and blue awning was stowed away against the side of the structure, secured with big nylon straps, but Lance could still make out the cutout for the entryway beneath its center. He looked across the area to his right. His direct line of sight was blocked by the fried Oreo stand (*Come on, Marcus. Get out here with your guys*), but flashlights were throwing shadows behind it, along with the occasional word or chuckle from a person.

He couldn't tell where exactly the people were, whether they'd be able to see him or not. He weighed his options. He could stand up straight and walk slowly and casually, like he belonged, and maybe in the dark nobody would be able to tell they didn't recognize him or what he was up to.

Or...

Lance took a deep breath and ran as fast as he could down the side of the truck and then the fun house, sliding so hard in the grass as he came to a stop that his legs nearly went out from under him. To keep himself upright, he reached out and grabbed the first thing he could touch, which happened to be a padlock.

A padlock securing the closed door to the fun house.

Lance reached out and touched the door, pushed, and it gave a little, warping under his pressure. Plywood at best, cheap, painted red like

(*Blood*)

the red stripes on the awning and the big shiny noses on the painted clowns. He looked around the door frame for hinges. Didn't see any.

It swings inward, he thought. *Should I...*

He knew what he had to do, but the noise would surely catch the attention of somebody. This close now, the coldness was digging deeper into him, and he fought to keep the sorrow that accompanied it from clouding his thoughts. He had to focus.

But wait. As he stared at the red door, something else

slithered through that coldness. Something sliced through the fog.

The buzzing at the base of his skull went off again. The hair on the back of his neck and on his arms stood up.

(You!)

A voice hissed in his head. A serpent's tongue in his ear.

That was all it took, just that one word, delivered by an established connection between Lance and whatever Darkness the voice belonged to, for Lance to instantly know this was the same force that had created the connection with him for Chrissy's dying moments all those years ago. The force that had taunted him without ever having to speak. Teased him, tormented him with the final moments of his classmate, forced him to live with the truth of her being dead and never being able to tell anyone or do anything about it.

(You can't stop us! You're pathetic! Worthless!)

Lance grinned in the dark. Whispered, "You have no idea what I am."

He took two steps back, lowered his shoulder, and then sprang forward, crashing into the padlocked door.

∼

THE WOOD SPLINTERED with Lance's impact, the latch and padlock falling to the ground, lost in the grass. A loud *THUD! and a* CRACK! and Lance was in, his momentum tumbling him forward. He lost his footing as the door burst open and he tripped over the raised lip of the threshold, falling onto his knees, reaching out with his hands to break his fall. He grunted as he hit the ground, then sprang back up, twisting around to look back out the doorway, braced to fend off an attacker.

But nobody was coming. The clouds above the carnival grounds rolled away and a sliver of moon cast a metallic glow across the fried Oreo booth, but Lance saw no movement headed his direction.

Not yet, he told himself. *But they're coming.* Then, *It knows I'm here now.*

He turned around again and stared at a solid black wall with a giant red arrow pointing to his left. Lance went left and was immediately met with pitch black. He pulled Leah's small flashlight from his pocket and clicked the button on its bottom to switch it on.

Nothing happened.

Lance clicked and clicked the button a few more times and finally the light fluttered for a moment and then stayed on, dull, but enough to get by with.

Lance made a mental note to buy batteries the next time he went into town.

With his weak beam of light guiding his way, Lance closed his eyes and took in a deep breath, the air a mixture of disinfectant and paint and traces of body odor—it reminded him of the high school locker room. The atmosphere felt thick and cloying, and he was already getting hot. He pushed up the sleeves of his sweatshirt and then took another deep breath, tried to settle his mind and focus, tune into whatever pulled him forward.

Which, he realized, wasn't exactly necessary. There was only one path through this fun house, and somewhere ahead lie the Maze of Mirrors.

Outside, a loud screeching sound followed by a heavy metal bang caused Lance to jump.

"Dammit, Felix!" an angry voice shouted. "You lost all your damn sense?"

Lance didn't wait to hear Felix's reply. He moved deeper into the structure.

First, the Clown Hall, which was nothing more than a narrow hallway with what looked like hundreds of framed pictures of clowns filling the walls on either side. Lance saw speakers in the upper corners, and several recessed lights in the ceiling and beneath the plexiglass floor, and imagined that when the fun house was powered on and functional, the hall would feel much more alive, much more *fun*, but in the quiet of night with just his dim flashlight, it seemed more like a sad shrine to hundreds of deceased clowns. Lance felt surrounded by the faces of clown corpses, their eyes open and locked onto him as he moved.

Even he had to admit it was damn creepy.

He moved faster.

The Upside-Down Room was a large square space with a bunch of living room furniture mounted to the carpeted ceiling. More soundless speakers and dead lights. A life-sized clown mannequin sat with its legs crossed in an upside-down recliner, an ear-to-ear smile on its face that looked sinister in Lance's flashlight beam. Lance eyed the clown cautiously as he passed beneath it. He felt silly, but he didn't care.

The Tilted Corner, which was just a slanted floor covered in a textured, grippy material, the walls lined with metal handrails for safety, led to the moving staircase, which, as far as Lance could tell, was just a regular staircase leading up a little way to the fun house's second story. But studying the walls briefly as he climbed, they appeared to be screens of some sort, maybe for a projector hidden somewhere above. Lance supposed there was usually some sort of illusion, a trick of the eye happening here when the place was juiced up, but tonight the whole place felt more like a boring haunted house.

He reached the top of the non-moving Moving Staircase and stopped.

He looked directly at himself, the muted light from his flashlight reflecting into his own face, making him squint.

He was looking into a mirror.

I'm here, he thought.

He stepped forward, and watched as his image suddenly filled the surrounding space from every angle, reflections on top of reflections. He was surrounded by mirrors.

"Tell you what, guys," he said to all the hims. "If we split up, this might go faster."

None of the hims answered.

Which, if he was being honest, was the best outcome.

He reached out with the hand not holding the flashlight and felt along the wall, making his way forward and feeling for a corner, some indication to make a turn. His fingers found the edge, wrapped around it. Lance leaned to the side and aimed the flashlight down the next corridor. Saw his own head reflected a dozen or more times, shrinking in size down the hallway. He rounded the corner and...

The flashlight went out.

Blackness swallowed him.

"Well, guys, that's some really bad timing, yeah?"

More so now than before, Lance was happy none of the hims answered back. His own voice speaking to him from the pitch-black darkness wasn't something he needed to deal with at the moment.

He clicked the button on the bottom of the flashlight over and over. The *click click click click* echoing around him. Nothing happened. Not even the tiniest hopeful pinprick of light.

Lance sighed. Reached out with his hand again and felt along the walls. Was about to take a step when a wave of freezing air crashed upon him. His skin prickled with goosebumps, he sucked in an icy breath. And then the air seemed to ... vibrate. A steady hum of energy that reminded Lance of...

The porch light.

His flashlight beam burst to life. Stronger than before. The hallway lit up bright, and Lance nearly screamed.

From a single mirror to his left, Chrissy Steel stared at him. Their eyes locked, and before Lance could speak, she waved for him to follow as she moved on to the next mirror, and then the next, making her way down the hallway through the individual pieces of glass. A lone Chrissy chased by a dozen hims as Lance followed.

The flashlight beam wavered as he moved, dimming as she got further away, brightening as Lance caught up. They made a right turn, and then a quick left, followed by another quick right. Lance felt dizzy, disoriented—unsure if it was because of the mirrors or the fog of death he could feel growing heavier as he went deeper into the mirror maze.

How many? He found himself asking as Chrissy continued on. *How many has it killed here?*

Lance followed Chrissy's ghost in the mirrors into a disorienting U-turn, which momentarily trapped him in a square of glass, reflecting himself in a full 360 degrees, as well as above him at all angles with slanted glass panels. It was like being trapped in a spider's eye. It was in this semi-encasement that Chrissy stopped moving. She chose the mirror that was in the center of the U-turn as a patron would pass through, mostly hidden from view from anyone yet to reach the square.

Lance stopped, turned to face her. The flashlight beam began to waver again as Chrissy's eyes bore into his from behind the glass. He could see concentration on her face, her eyes squinting. The flashlight flickered. Went out.

(Here)

Chrissy's voice struck him in the dark.

Her image in the mirror began to glow a soft blue, just the faintest outline. Enough for Lance to make out the vague shape of her, head and torso and limbs.

He watched as Chrissy raised an arm and then held out her hand, pressing her palm flat against the glass, fingers splayed.

Instinctively, Lance found himself raising his own hand, aligning it with hers against his side of the mirror. His reflection overlapping hers, palm to palm. He waited for something to happen—a connection, a vision, *anything*.

But nothing did.

In a flash, Chrissy was gone again, and Lance was left once more in the black, his palm still pressed to the mirror. He waited. He thought. He clicked the flashlight button again, but still, no dice.

Here. But what's *here?*

Sounds from below. Maybe nothing. But maybe something. Enough to make him want to get going. But no, he couldn't. Not yet.

Here...

Right here...

"What if..."

Lance pushed on the glass, testing its strength. The mirror held firm, but the entire panel shifted the tiniest bit beneath his weight.

He pushed harder. Felt more give this time.

The third time, he really leaned into it, and the entire panel sank back maybe an inch before Lance heard a heavy spring release. When he let go of the mirror, the panel popped back toward him further than before. He felt along the edge, found the small gap that had been created, and pulled.

The mirror swung outward on silent hinges. It wasn't just a mirror. It was a door.

∽

LANCE STEPPED BACK, pulling the mirror-door open all the way, revealing a black rectangle of an opening, a dead tooth in a row of polished ones. The blackness in the opening seemed vast, as if nothing existing beyond it, a portal to another dimension.

But the overwhelming sense of dread that poured from the opening told Lance that things did exist beyond it. Terrible things had happened on the other side of the mirrored walls. The sense of *fear* was suffocating. The trapped essence of terrified souls poured out toward him, their savior come at last.

Lance pushed against the wall of sorrow that came at him, moved forward into that blackened tooth of an opening, feeling his way, blindly groping the walls with his palms. Just across the threshold, the air grew cooler, but the horror increased. His head filled with screams and cries, voices begging and pleading.

"I'm here," Lance managed to choke out, emotion tightening his throat. "I'm here."

He could feel them now. Chrissy and all the others, so many others. He saw their faces in his mind as he felt their spirits coalesce around him, using him as a beacon, a light they could gather round.

He could feel the energy growing stronger as they came close. They reached for him, desperate to cling to his power. Maybe it was because of their personal connection, however small it had been, but Chrissy's was the first soul to join him in the ether of time and space which he'd opened himself to, reached his helping hand into. The moment their energies connected, the flashlight beam exploded to life again, brighter than ever. It hummed and vibrated in his hand.

Lace opened his eyes, now able to see the hidden space behind the mirror for the first time. There was nothing but rough wooden walls and a wooden floor. In the floor a large trapdoor was inset. Its hinges and the padlocked latch looked shiny and new, probably replaced often. The wood used here was much stronger than the wood used for the fun house door Lance had easily broken through.

That's where he keeps them, Lace thought. *He snatches them from the maze and takes them down there and...*

"You must really want to fucking die."

A hoarse and phlegmy voice from behind him.

Lance spun, the flashlight beam illuminating the face of a man standing just a couple feet outside the opened mirror-door. The man was tall, taller than Lance by at least two inches, with thick, broad shoulders and powerful-looking arms that ended in hands that looked as though they could rip phone books in half. He wore faded and worn-out blue jeans with heavy work boots and a blue and red flannel shirt. He looked to be middle-aged, maybe in his forties, and his deeply tanned face was covered in splotches of black whiskers.

Lance took all this in within two seconds, but these attributes were not the things he cared about.

The first thing Lance focused on was the large hunting knife the man held gripped in one of those catcher-mitt hands. The blade was at least eight inches. Sharp point at the top, partially serrated along its length.

He'll gut me with that, Lance thought. *Or slice my throat. He'll do either and not think twice about it.*

Lance knew the man wouldn't think twice about it, because he could see that the thing he was looking at was not a man at all—not entirely.

Lance had felt the Evil inside this man—this *murderer*—all those years ago when Chrissy had died, and he'd felt again earlier, when it had found him about to break into the fun house, called him pathetic and worthless. Lance had felt it those times, but now he could *see* it.

Though a human man stood in front of him, the images in the mirrors all around the man showed not a reflection of himself, but his *true* self. The Evil that fed on his mind and soul, controlled him. The thing that had really killed Chrissy Steel and all the others.

The creature in the mirrors was as tall as the man, but thinner, lankier. It had no skin, but instead looked like a human who'd been peeled down to nothing but muscle and sinew, black and grey and rotted. Its arms were gangly, hanging down low, fingertips spiked with talons nearly touching its knees. A bulbous and uneven head, an eye the size of a saucer where a nose should be, with three tiny eyes above, all blinking out of turn. It had no mouth.

At the sight of the thing, Lance felt a stirring in the part of his mind he'd left open to the ether. He felt the girls there, seeing the thing too, and he felt their *anger*.

And with it, his own anger blossomed. He choked it down. Had to keep himself under control. For them.

Lance finally spoke. "I'd prefer not to die tonight, actually."

I'm here, he thought. *Come to me. Use me.*

The girls' anger began to morph into something else. He could feel a new understanding come over them. A few more latched on, and the flashlight flickered and then grew brighter still.

The thing in the mirror focused all its eyes on Lance as it blinked erratically. Lance watched as the man with the knife jerked and then stood ramrod straight. The cords in his neck bulged and his lips started to squirm and his cheeks puffed, like he was swishing mouth wash. His eyes went wide, and his mouth opened and a rush of hot air gushed out along with hissing words—words from the beast in the mirror, delivered by its puppet.

"I know of you. They say you are strong, but to me, you appear weak and stupid. I will take great pleasure in being the one to end you. I will be rewarded." Then, because Evil can never help itself. "You couldn't save her then. She begged for somebody to help her, and you heard her cries but you failed. Let that be your last thought before you die, before I feast on your soul."

The flashlight began to hum loudly in Lance's hand. He breathed in deep, feeling the swell of energy. Fed it with his fuel, reached into his well and let them drink as much as they needed, as much as they *wanted*. A cosmic joining of forces.

He felt his head begin to throb, felt his heart begin to beat too fast, yet he stayed strong. His vision began to jitter. He could not continue to let things build a moment longer.

"Hey," Lance said. "Remember when I said you had no idea what I am? I meant that. But the thing is, it's not me you have to worry about."

There was a ZAP! of static in the air and the flashlight went out.

And Lance released them.

Go.

A new light source fired to life in the mirrored space, a bright blue glow that flickered like flames, surrounded the man. His eyes blinked in confusion and he stumbled back a few steps, crashing into the mirror behind him, the only mirror which still held the image of the skinless creature.

Surrounding both the man and the demon inside him, inside each of the other mirrors was the spirit of a different girl. Girls of all different races and sizes. All young—early twenties at the most. All victims.

And the man could see them. He screamed as they leaned in closer, their shapes growing large and looming in the glass. They stood tall over him, the blue light pulsing, streaked with flashes of red. The man screamed again and shrank down to the floor. "Get away! Get away from me!"

The girls turned their heads all at once, gazes snapping to the creature trapped in its single mirror. Its grotesque eyes darted in all different directions, trying to see them all at once, before it finally looked back to Lance. The thing couldn't convey much emotion with its limited features, but Lance liked to think he saw disbelief on the creature's face right before the girls ripped it apart.

Their arms reached into the demon's mirror and it tried to shrink away from their touch to no avail. They groped and grabbed and piled into its space, crowding it as the thing cowered away. With their newfound strength they tore its limbs off, twisted appendages, snapped its neck, all while that blue light pulsed faster and brighter, the red sparking like a firework. And as they tore the creature apart, destroying the evil that had robbed their families and friends of them, robbed them of their future, Lance watched as the man on the floor jerked and twisted and spasmed, flailing about like the victim of a Voodoo doll, or a man eaten alive by unseen flames.

And then it was over.

The blue light stopped pulsing and dimmed down low. The creature in the mirror, now in pieces, those eyes blinking no more, faded away like wisps of smoke caught in the wind.

The girls—those poor, poor girls—stood back in their mirrors and looked at Lance. He took them all in, looked them each in their eyes, giving them each the respect they deserved.

"I'm so sorry for what happened to you," he said. Then, "You're free now."

The blue light vanished, darkness blanketing everything once more.

Lance collapsed to the floor, depleted, succumbing to his own blackness.

Right before he was completely gone, he saw Chrissy Steel's face one last time.

She smiled.

∽

KENDALL BEUFORD CRANSTON, age forty-three, suffered a massive heart-attack that night in the Maze of Mirrors, which nearly killed him.

Nearly.

Marcus Johnston and a veteran sheriff's deputy named Paul Score had found Lance and Kendall on the floor of the darkened fun house just three minutes after the ghosts of the lost girls had gotten revenge and then their freedom to pass on to whatever waited for them beyond. By the time the paramedics arrived, Lance was coming to, and Marcus hooked Lance's arm over his shoulder for support and ushered him out of the fun house as quickly as he could while all the medical attention was being paid to Kendall Cranston.

"He killed them all," Lance said, his voice barely above a whisper. "Chrissy and others."

Marcus nodded and patted Lance's chest. "I'm sure he did," he said. "Now we just have to prove it."

After Lance assured Marcus he'd be okay, that he just needed some coffee and some food, Marcus helped him into Leah's Beetle and she drove him home.

By the time they arrived at the house, Lance was already

feeling a little better, his body restoring itself after its exertion. He sat at the kitchen table and drank a full pot of coffee and ate an entire box of frozen waffles with butter and syrup, all while telling Leah everything that had happened inside the fun house.

"*Amazing*," she said. "Talk about girl power, huh? Good for them. I'm glad they'll finally have some peace." Then she reached out a hand and laid it atop his as he forked a bit of waffle into his mouth. "Were you scared?" she asked. "He could have killed you."

Lance swallowed. Shook his head. "I was angry."

She sat back in her chair. "Angry?"

Lance pulled his hand free and then took his plate to the sink. Turned and leaned against the counter, crossed his arms. "I looked at all those girls, and I saw you in each and every one of them. Smart, strong, beautiful." A beat. "It could have been you, Leah. A different time and a different place and you might have been the one going through that fun house, the one he would choose that night."

She stared at him. Waited for more.

He never broke eye contact as he said, "If those girls hadn't ripped that thing to pieces, I would have ripped *him* apart."

Leah stared at him a moment more, then stood from the table and hugged him, burying her face in his chest. He wrapped his arms around her, pulling her even closer, becoming one.

Finally, the hug broke, and life continued.

"Come on," Leah said, walking out of the kitchen. "Let's go to bed."

"The sun will be up in like an hour," Lance said.

Leah stopped halfway across the living room. Turned and gave him a look that was unmistakable. "Are you saying no to me, Lance Brody?"

Lance said nothing.

He followed her.

∼

THREE HOURS LATER, Marcus Johnston knocked on their front door. Leah let him in, and Lance made more coffee. They sat around the table with the morning sunlight streaming through the kitchen windows and Marcus sipped his first sip and said to Lance, "Turns out it wasn't all that hard to prove the guy killed Chrissy and the rest of them. He confessed to everything."

Marcus told them that the doctors said it was touch and go for a while, but somehow Kendall Beuford Cranston managed to pull through. Once he was conscious again, it all just started pouring out of him, like a dam had broken and the lifetime of secrets and sins it'd been holding back broke free, impossible to stop. The doctors immediately called the sheriff, who called Marcus, and together the two men arrived at the hospital and Kendall Beuford Cranston told them everything again, over and over and over, like a broken record, a repeat loop of confessed transgressions.

"I've already got a call in to the FBI," Marcus said. "So far, Cranston has confessed to abducting and murdering fourteen young girls across the United States. He knew exactly where each one had been buried when he was finished with them."

"*Fourteen?*" Leah gasped.

Marcus nodded, looking glum. "Best we can tell—his timeline's a little hard to follow so far—the murders were spaced out over the last twenty years or so. The guy's father confirmed that sounded about right?"

"His father?" Lance asked.

"Yep. Vernon Cranston. Guy's eighty. From Kansas originally. A real talker. Said he's been traveling the country and working *shows*, that's how he put it, since he was ten. He and Kendall own and operate the fun house. And get this, the guy said he's always, and I'm quoting here, 'Always known his boy had some wires loose, but hoped one day they'd tighten up.' Can you believe that BS? He acted like murdering over a dozen young women was nothing more than a personality quirk."

Lance thought back to that morning he and Marcus had tried to save Chrissy, how she'd seemed to get further away as she'd been tormented and killed. Later, he'd figured there must have been two people involved, and now he could see it all in his head: Kendall doing awful things to Chrissy in that hidden room in the back of the fun house, all while his father drove the big F-350 out of town, towing his Evil-possessed son behind him.

"He's locked up, right? The father?" Leah asked.

Marcus nodded. "Sheriff's got him in custody, yes." Then he sighed and leaned back in his chair, looking almost defeated, somber. Asked Lance, "Remember what the Lewis kid told us back then? How he'd asked Chrissy to meet him at the carnival if she didn't go to the party?"

Lance nodded. All the pieces fit now.

"Guess that was always our answer, huh?" Marcus said. "Chrissy left home, and walked to the carnival—it was only, what, a little less than two miles from her house?—and got taken. Never saw the Lewis kid." He shook his head. "I don't know if she actually went into the fun house alone, or if maybe the Cranston guy grabbed her somewhere else and stowed her away there..." He trailed off.

Lance knew Marcus was feeling the same things Lance had been feeling for years, a sense of letting Chrissy down.

"We can't change it, Marcus. But we've finally done the only thing we can do now. We've caught the monster, and we can start to offer closure to all those girls' families."

They drank their coffee and Leah asked Marcus if he was hungry. He said he was starving, actually, and Leah offered to make him breakfast. "Anything except waffles," she said.

As Leah worked on making Marcus an omelette, Marcus finished his coffee and looked at Lance. Said, "Can you explain to me why this guy's suddenly spewing his lifetime's worth of crimes? It can't just be the heart-attack, right? I mean, you should see the guy, Lance. He's squirrelly. His eyes are wide open all the time, and he keeps looking all around him like something's about to jump out and grab him. He can't hold still. I swear, it's like he's seen a ghost."

From the stove, Leah laughed.

Lance couldn't help but grin big, reaching for Marcus's coffee mug to refill it.

"What?" Marcus asked, confused.

Lance shrugged. "Maybe he did, Marcus. Maybe he did."

AUTHOR'S NOTE

Thanks so much for reading **Dark Return**. I hope you enjoyed it. If you *did* enjoy it and have a few minutes to spare, I would greatly appreciate it if you could leave a review saying so. Reviews help authors more than you can imagine, and help readers like you find more great books to read. Win-win!

Thanks again for reading, and take care!

-Michael Robertson Jr

For all the latest info, including release dates, giveaways, and special events, sign up for the Michael Robertson, Jr. VIP Readers List. As a Thank You, you'll also receive a FREE audiobook and ebook. (He promises to never spam you!)

http://mrobertsonjr.com/newsletter-sign-up

More from Michael Robertson Jr

LANCE BRODY SERIES

Dark Choice (Book 7)

Dark Holiday (Book 6)

Dark Rest (Book 5.5 - Short Story)

Dark Woods (Book 5)

Dark Vacancy (Book 4)

Dark Shore (Book 3)

Dark Deception (Book 2.5 - Short Story)

Dark Son (Book 2)

Dark Game (Book 1)

Dark Beginnings (Book 0 - Prequel Novella)

SHIFFY P.I. SERIES

Prey No More (Book 2)

Run No More (Book 1)

OTHER NOVELS

The End House

Cedar Ridge

Transit

Rough Draft (A Kindle #1 Horror Bestseller!)

Regret*

Collections

Tormented Thoughts: Tales of Horror

The Teachers' Lounge*

*Writing as Dan Dawkins

Follow On:

Facebook.com/mrobertsonjr

Mrobertsonjr.substack.com

Instagram.com/mrobertsonjr

Printed in Great Britain
by Amazon